YOU ARE CA ████████████████

Suddenly the g██████████████████ nd
the crowd surge █████████████████ nd
Irena quickly unfurl their banner and run up to
the front of the marching column, each holding
a supporting pole with the banner stretched out
between.

You march into the city, side by side with Sergei, Irena, and the Bolsheviks. Suddenly you
hear pops like firecrackers from the rooftops.
People start falling to the ground all around you.
There are screams as some members of the
crowd scatter, dashing for cover in the doorways
of the buildings along the street. Others, heads
held high and fists upraised, keep marching.

Sergei suddenly gasps and grabs his chest,
blood flowing out between his fingers. He drops
his end of the banner and sinks to his knees.
With bullets pinging on the pavement all around
you, you and Irena get Sergei up off the street
and into a protected doorway....

You want to help your friend, but you're also
trapped by the sharpshooters on the roofs. What
will you do?

**ONLY *YOU*, AS YOUNG INDIANA JONES,
CAN DECIDE...**

Bantam Books in the Choose Your Own Adventure® series
Ask your bookseller for the books you have missed

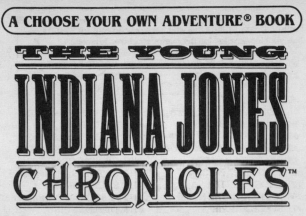

A CHOOSE YOUR OWN ADVENTURE® BOOK

THE YOUNG INDIANA JONES CHRONICLES™

Book 3

REVOLUTION IN RUSSIA

PETROGRAD, July 1917

By Richard Brightfield

Adapted from the television episode
"Petrograd, July 1917"
Teleplay by Gavin Scott
Story by George Lucas

Illustrated by Frank Bolle

BANTAM BOOKS
NEW YORK • TORONTO • LONDON • SYDNEY • AUCKLAND

RL 5, age 10 and up

REVOLUTION IN RUSSIA
A Bantam Book / September 1992

CHOOSE YOUR OWN ADVENTURE® is a registered trademark of Bantam Books, a division of Bantam Doubleday Dell Publishing Group, Inc.
Registered in U.S. Patent and Trademark Office and elsewhere.
Original conception of Edward Packard

THE YOUNG INDIANA JONES CHRONICLES™
is a trademark of Lucasfilm Ltd.
All rights reserved. Used under authorization.

Cover art by George Tsui
Interior illustrations by Frank Bolle

ISBN 0-553-29784-8

Published simultaneously in the United States and Canada

Bantam Books are published by Bantam Books, a division of Bantam Doubleday Dell Publishing Group, Inc. Its trademark, consisting of the words "Bantam Books" and the portrayal of a rooster, is Registered in U.S. Patent and Trademark Office and in other countries. Marca Registrada. Bantam Books, 666 Fifth Avenue, New York, New York 10103.

PRINTED IN THE UNITED STATES OF AMERICA

OPM   0 9 8 7 6 5 4 3 2 1

REVOLUTION
IN RUSSIA

Your Adventure

The year is 1917. You are young Indiana Jones, the son of a professor of medieval studies at Princeton University in New Jersey. In this book you are traveling through Russia, working as an undercover spy for the French embassy.

In the adventures that follow, you will get to meet many famous figures in history, such as Vladimir Lenin, leader of the Bolshevik Revolution. You will also experience life during the revolution and learn firsthand all about political science and comparative political philosophies. You may even join in an attempt to overthrow the provisional government and play an important role in how the people of Russia will be ruled.

From time to time as you read along, you will be asked to make a choice. The adventures you have as Indiana Jones are the results of your choices. You are responsible because you choose. After you make your decision, follow the instructions to find out what happens to you next. Remember, your Russian adventures depend on the actions you decide to take.

To help you in your travels, a special glossary is provided at the end of the book.

Chronology

August 1, 1914—The First World War starts with Germany's declaration of war on Russia.

March 6, 1917—The czar abdicates in Russia. A provisional government takes over.

April 6, 1917—The United States declares war on Germany.

April 10, 1917—Lenin is back in Petrograd and meets with Trotsky and Stalin to discuss strategy.

June 16, 1917—Kerensky, the minister of war under the provisional government, debates Lenin in public. Kerensky advocates continuing the war. Lenin advocates peace.

June 27, 1917—General Pershing and the first American troops arrive in France. His officers are veterans of the pursuit of Pancho Villa in Mexico.

July 3, 1917—Widespread rioting breaks out in Petrograd as Bolshevik supporters, against the advice of Lenin, try to stage a coup d'état.

July 17, 1917—Lenin escapes as Kerensky crushes another Bolshevik demonstration.

July 20, 1917—Kerensky assumes the premiership of Russia and orders an immediate military offensive against the Germans, with disastrous consequences for the Russians.

November 7, 1917 (October 25 by the Russian calendar)—The Bolsheviks seize power.

You are Indiana Jones. You were born on July 1, 1899 in Princeton, New Jersey, where your father is a professor of medieval studies at the university. It is now 1917, and you are seventeen years old.

The First World War is raging in Europe, and the United States has entered the war against Germany. You have just finished working as an agent for a secret anti-German spy network stationed in neutral Spain. At the moment, you are in Barcelona, in a café across the street from the colorful, unfinished cathedral designed by Antonio Gaudi. You are with Charles, one of your fellow spies. He is with French Intelligence, and he has a proposition for you.

"My commander has asked me to find a good agent for him," Charles says. "And you, *mon ami*, are perfect."

"I appreciate your confidence," you say. "But my country has just entered the war and—"

→ → → → → → → → → → → → →
Turn to page 2.

2

"But this is very important, for your country as well as mine. Maybe the most important job of the war," Charles says.

"Then why don't you take the job yourself?" you ask.

"I wish I could," Charles says, "but, *quel dommage*, it is a pity that I must complete a secret mission here. And also, I do not speak Russian the way you do."

"Russian? Did you say Russian?"

"That is right, the assignment is in Russia," Charles says, leaning over to whisper. "More specifically, in Petrograd, the capital."

"But I thought the Russians were on our side."

"That's the problem," Charles says, motioning for you to keep your voice down in case others are listening. "The czar has fallen, and a provisional government has taken over. The country is in a state of chaos. A group called the Bolsheviks may seize control and try to take Russia out of the war. Then German forces there can be sent to fight both our countries. French Intelligence wants to try to prevent this from happening."

"I see your point," you say. "Under the circumstances, I guess I have no choice. You've convinced me. I'll give it a try."

"*Splendide!*" Charles exclaims.

"One little point," you say. "How do I get to Russia?"

"That will be no problem," Charles says. "You can go either by the northern route through Finland, or a southern one through Greece, Serbia, and Romania. Then across Russia to Petrograd, the capital."

"Which way do you think is best?" you ask.

"We have trusted agents in place in Greece and Romania. They can guide you through and provide safe houses for you to stay in."

"That sounds best," you say.

"But Serbia and Romania are very dangerous places. Plague is ravaging the countryside. Many of our agents have died there."

"And Finland?" you ask.

"Ah, the land of the midnight sun. Of course you will have to go by ship to Sweden first and risk attack by submarine. The Germans are sinking ships of all nations, even neutral ones. That is what brought your country into the war."

Oh great, you think. I risk dying of plague going by the southern route and could be torpedoed trying to get to Finland on the northern one.

→ → → → → → → → → → → →

Go on to the next page.

4

You sit back in your seat, trying to make your decision.

→ → → → → → → → → → → →

If you decide to take the northern route by way of Finland, turn to page 62.

If you decide to take the southern route by way of Greece, Serbia, and Romania, turn to page 86.

You decide to take the rest of the day off. You spend it walking around the city, marveling at its wide boulevards and splendid buildings.

It's late afternoon when you get back to the Red Palace. The door to Sergei and Irena's apartment is open, and you can hear Sergei practicing a speech. You listen for a few minutes, then knock on the side of the door.

"Come in," Sergei says, "I was just getting ready for tomorrow night. Irena and I are planning to speak at several rallies. I may also get to use my banner—maybe at the Putilov Steelworks."

"Sounds like you and the Bolsheviks are getting ready to make your move."

"I wish it were true," Sergei says.

→ → → → → → → → → → → → →
Turn to page 63.

Upon your arrival at the hotel, you spread out the material from Charles's envelope on your bed. There's a map of your route, train schedules, and several bundles of money in the currencies of the different countries you'll be passing through. There's also a list of code words that you memorize. Your code name in French Intelligence is now Captain Defense. Afterward, you burn the paper the codes are written on.

The next train going across the mountains to France is scheduled to leave from the Estación de Francia in an hour. You decide to try to make it.

You quickly pack and check out of the hotel. Then you take a taxi to the train station. Despite the war going on in most of Europe, it's packed with tourists and vacationers.

You buy a ticket for Bayonne, a major seaport on the other side of the mountains on the French coast. Then you work your way through the crowd to the track where your train is ready to depart. You climb aboard, continuing down the corridor to your compartment.

You hear several blasts of the train whistle outside, and after a slight jolt, the train begins to move slowly.

At the same moment, the door to your compartment opens, and a young woman about your age steps in.

→ → → → → → → → → → → →

Go on to the next page.

8

The woman is tall, blond, and very attractive. She smiles as she takes the seat next to you.

"Almost missed the train," she says, out of breath. She speaks English with a Scandinavian accent. "My name is Anita, Anita Johnson." She pronounces Johnson *Yahn-sun*. "I am glad to be riding with you. I am returning to Sweden from my vacation."

"I'm going to Sweden myself," you say. "To Russia actually, but to Sweden first."

"Good, we can be traveling companions for the trip," Anita says. "You go by ship also?"

"I was thinking of it."

"My uncle is the captain of a Swedish ship leaving from Bayonne. Perhaps you would want to go with us?"

"That sounds like a good idea," you say. "Can I—"

"Now I sleep," she interrupts. "I have been up all night at parties for the past three nights. Those Spanish at the coastal resorts really know how to live."

Anita closes her eyes and seems to go immediately to sleep.

You sit quietly and read, every so often gazing out the window at the passing countryside.

As it starts to get dark, the train begins rising up into the mountains. The ranges of snowy peaks around you still glow with pink light long after the valleys through which you are traveling have grown dark.

Early the next day, you arrive in France at Toulouse, a small city of narrow streets and high, redbrick towers. You and Anita, now both rested, change trains for the ride to the coast.

Your compartment quickly fills up with vacationers—five more adults and three children—going to the Atlantic beaches for the summer. You notice that there are no men of military age, just grandparents and young children. More than likely the men are off to war.

At sunset, the train pulls into the Bayonne station.

"I have arranged to meet my uncle, Captain Gustav, at a café along the Place de la Liberté not far from here," Anita says.

You follow her from the train station through the narrow streets to a wide square. One side is lined with open-air cafés.

Anita leads you to a café at the far end.

"Uncle Gustav should be here soon," she says as you sit down at one of the outdoor tables. "Oh, here he comes now."

→ → → → → → → → → → → → →
Go on to the next page.

A tall, pale-complexioned man sporting a blond beard and wearing a ship captain's cap appears out of the crowd and heads for your table. Anita jumps up. She and Gustav hug happily for a moment.

"This is someone from America I met on the train," she says, introducing you. "Do you think we can take my new friend to Sweden?"

Gustav looks hard at you with his pale blue eyes. "Yes, I think so. I like the Americans. We have relatives there in your state of Minnesota. But I must warn you, the voyage will have its dangers. The Germans are practicing unrestricted warfare. Their submarines are sinking any ship they can find on the high seas.

"Several months ago," Gustav continues, taking a seat, "the Germans torpedoed two American ships on the same day—while your country was still neutral. It was the day that the provisional government came to power in Russia, right after the czar was overthrown. A few weeks later, the United States had no choice but to declare war on Germany."

"You are following the situation in Russia very closely, I see," you say.

"Since they occupy Finland, they are our neighbors. What happens there affects us deeply. Right now there are two groups in Russia struggling for power, the provisional government, led by Kerensky, and the Bolsheviks, led by a man named Lenin. Lenin wants to make peace with the Germans. They transported him from Switzerland back to Russia in a sealed train."

"Now that the Americans are in the war," you say, "I don't think it's going to last much longer. Once General Pershing starts going after them, I think the Germans will be finished. I know General Pershing personally, and . . ."

Gustav pushes his chair away from the table and looks you over again, stroking his beard. "You either have a great imagination, or you are a most unusual person."

"I vote for unusual person," Anita says.

A boat's whistle blows twice somewhere in the distance. "That's the *Helmsfjord,*" Gustav says. "We'll walk to the ship."

Gustav leads you and Anita to the waterfront. It's a beehive of activity, lit up with floodlights. Huge piles of cargo are being loaded on dozens of ships.

→ → → → → → → → → → → →
Go on to the next page.

You and Anita follow Gustav up the gangplank to the deck of the *Helmsfjord*. You notice that the hull is painted with camouflage colors. A crew member then shows you to a small cabin where you stow your gear.

A short time later, shouts go up from one end of the ship to the other, as lines are cast off. The whistle blows again, this time much louder, since it's right over your head. The steam engine begins to throb somewhere below, and the deck vibrates under your feet.

The next morning finds you steaming north along the French coast—barely visible far off in the distance. Two other freighters camouflaged similarly to yours are not far away—one in front, and one behind. A small French destroyer steams alongside your miniature convoy.

You and Anita join Captain Gustav on the bridge, where you spend most of the voyage.

"Do you think there are any submarines out there?" you ask.

"One never knows," Gustav says. "But our escort destroyer is now equipped with depth charges and hydrophones to detect the sound of underwater propellers."

By late the next day, you are far up the coast and nearing the English Channel. "This is the most dangerous area," Gustav says. "Now we must watch our step."

→ → → → → → → → → → → → →

Go on to the next page.

There is a crackling of Morse code coming from the radio room behind the bridge. "Our escort has heard something. They're warning us to be on alert," Gustav says.

You quickly don your life preserver.

At the same time, you hear the throbbing sound of an aircraft engine somewhere in the distance. You shield your eyes against the setting sun and see a small, single-seater biplane approaching from the West.

"That's an English plane on coastal patrol," Gustav says. "I think this particular one is what they call a 'Sopwith Pup.'"

"That's a strange name for a plane," Anita says.

"Sopwith, I believe, refers to its designer, Sir Thomas Sopwith," Gustav says. "The 'Pup' may refer to its size, but I'm not sure."

The plane swoops low, passing overhead, and drops a flag marker on the water. The destroyer turns and heads in that direction. Seconds later, the side of the ship ahead of you erupts in flames.

"Oh, no!" Gustav shouts. "I know the captain of that ship. We'll stand by to pick up survivors."

The destroyer is now dropping depth charges around the spot marked by the plane. You see the gray bow of a submarine shoot vertically up out of the water, like a surfacing whale, and then sink back into the depths.

→ → → → → → → → → → → →

Go on to the next page.

"At least they got the submarine," Gustav says.

The plane waggles its wings and heads back toward the English coast as the deck of the torpedoed freighter up ahead sinks below the surface.

Your ship picks up several lifeboats full of survivors. Unfortunately, Gustav's friend is not among them. He has apparently gone down with his ship.

The mood of the rest of your trip is somber. Gustav keeps to himself, as you and the rest of the passengers care for the new arrivals.

Two days later, you dock in Stockholm, Sweden.

The city of Stockholm is festive with Midsummer Day celebrations—a time when there is only a brief period of semidarkness at night. The parks and gardens are riotously red with geraniums, petunias, and other flowers that grow profusely in the intense and prolonged light of the Scandinavian summer.

You thank Captain Gustav for his hospitality. Anita then takes you to a café beside one of the many canals that thread their way through the city. The café is crowded with English, Germans, Russians, Poles, Czechs, and Turks, all forgetting their hatreds for the moment and celebrating along with the neutral Swedes. You fill up a plate with pickled fish, salad, pâté, and slices of rye bread from a smorgasbord table at the side of the café.

While you are eating, Anita goes off and comes back with a lanky, blond-haired boy about your age. "I have a surprise for you," she says. "This is my brother, Olaf. He is a reporter for one of the Stockholm newspapers, and he is going to Petrograd tomorrow. He knows many people there. You can travel with him."

"It is all arranged," Olaf says. "Tonight we go by truck up the coast to Umeå. There we take a small boat across the Gulf of Bothnia to the town of Vaasa in Finland. From there a train will take us to St. Petersburg, or what the Russians now call Petrograd."

"Anita, Olaf ... I don't really know how to thank you," you say.

Anita laughs. "You made my trip home interesting for me. Maybe I'll see you again in Barcelona next year."

That night, you find yourself in the open back of a truck heading along a bumpy highway going north. Several times you see fireworks in the far distance as one town or another celebrates Midsummer Day. It is an eerie feeling to be riding along close to midnight and still be able to see clearly enough to read a newspaper in the dim light.

→ → → → → → → → → → → → →

Go on to the next page.

The next day, you are on a train in Finland, chugging across the endless stretches of dark fir and pine, punctuated by hundreds of lakes.

You ask Olaf what he knows about the situation in Petrograd. "All we hear in Stockholm are rumors," he says. "One day I hear that what's left of the czar's army has moved into Petrograd and executed the entire provisional government as well as all the revolutionaries, restoring the czar to power. The next day I hear that the Bolsheviks have taken over and executed everyone else. That is why I have to go back to Russia to find out what is actually happening."

"Do you think the Bolsheviks can actually seize power?" you ask.

"I hear that they are well organized and that many of the workers and soldiers support them. But I wouldn't count the reactionary forces out. They are very strong and still control the cossacks. The situation could go either way."

At noon your train pulls into the Finland Station in Petrograd. The station is packed. Welcoming committees are there to greet revolutionaries returning to Russia. Cheers go up as they step from the train. The station is also crowded with soldiers returning from the front, most of them deserters camping out in the station itself. Many of them have removed the imperial brass buttons from their uniforms and are wearing red armbands to show their support for the Bolsheviks. In every corner of the station, orators are shouting out their radical political platforms to the milling crowds.

As you and Olaf leave the station, you see that there are no buildings burning and no cossacks charging.

You thank Olaf for helping you get here.

"You're welcome," he says. "I'll be at the Bearpit Café if you want to meet up with me later. I can tell you what I've learned."

"Do you have any idea where the French embassy is?" you ask him.

→ → → → → → → → → → → →
Go on to the next page.

"Sure, follow me," Olaf says.

The two of you dash into the street and hop aboard a double streetcar just passing the station. In contrast to the crowds and ragged soldiers in the station, the people aboard the streetcar seem well dressed.

"All these people are either going to the theater or the ballet," Olaf says.

"While the revolution is going on?" you say.

"I guess they want to take their minds off what's happening," he says.

After a number of blocks, Olaf points up ahead to a large, imposing building. "There's your French embassy," he says. "I'm staying on the tram. Meet me at the Bearpit Café tonight. It's where all the young revolutionaries hang out."

You thank Olaf again and hop off the still-moving streetcar. As you approach the front door of the embassy, a guard in full dress uniform stops you and asks for your papers. You show him the pass you got from Charles.

"Good," he says. "Monsieur Laurentine has been expecting you. I will take you to his office."

Laurentine's office is cavernous, with an oversize desk. Monsieur Laurentine himself is an elegantly dressed, shrewd-looking little man wearing gold-rimmed eyeglasses clipped to his nose with a spring.

→ → → → → → → → → → → → →
Go on to the next page.

"Ah, Captain Defense," Laurentine says, calling you by your code name as you enter his office. He seems to recognize you at once. "You have arrived none too soon. Things are happening thick and fast. Come, we'll go right to the operations room."

You follow Laurentine out of his office and down a long hallway. At the end, a wide staircase descends to a lower level. There a side door opens into a narrow circular stairway that leads down to a tiny basement room packed with files and heaps of documents. Almost buried in this accumulation is a very thin young man wearing thick, wire-rimmed glasses.

"I'd like you to meet our station analyst, Monsieur Brossard," Laurentine says. "The two of you will be working closely together."

Brossard tries to get up to shake hands but only manages to knock over a tall pile of documents.

"Your desk, Captain Defense, is over there in the corner."

You look over and see nothing but stacks of papers. "A desk... where?" you ask, working your way toward the corner.

"No matter, you'll be out in the field most of the time. Brossard will hold down the fort here."

"I think the Bolsheviks will make their move soon," Brossard says.

"Are you sure?" Laurentine asks.

→ → → → → → → → → → → →
Go on to the next page.

"Fairly sure," Brossard says. "Lenin is giving a speech tonight at a meeting of the Bolsheviks in Keshinskiya Palace. The tone of the speech might give us some definite information."

"This can be your first assignment, Captain Defense," Laurentine says.

"It could," you say. "But I also have a contact at the Bearpit Café. I'm told that all the young Bolsheviks congregate there. It might be a good place for me to find out what's happening."

"Yes, the Bearpit Café. I've heard of it. A hotbed of young radicals," Laurentine says. "Well, I'll leave it up to you, Captain Defense. You can't cover both places at the same time."

This could be a good chance to see Lenin in person, you think. You've certainly heard a lot about him. On the other hand, you're itching to see this café that Olaf has told you about.

It's a hard choice, you think, as you try to find a path through the piles of papers leading back to the door of the basement room.

→ → → → → → → → → → → →

If you decide to hear Lenin's speech, turn to page 91.

If you decide to go to the Bearpit Café, turn to page 54.

Later that afternoon, you pick up your bag from the embassy cloakroom and head back toward the Red Palace. You go over to the wide Neva River and walk along the embankment. You are almost to the apartment complex when you meet Dmitri and Rosa coming from the opposite direction.

"This is great," Rosa tells you. "There's something I really want to show you."

"I'm taking my things over to the palace," you say. "I'd like to get them stowed away and—"

"Dmitri will take your bag over for you," Rosa says.

"I'd be glad to," Dmitri says.

"But—" you start to protest as Dmitri grabs your bag and heads toward the apartments. At the same time, Rosa starts leading you in the direction you just came from.

"It's just around the corner," Rosa says.

After several blocks, she stops in front of a small, humpbacked bridge across one of the many canals that lead off the Neva.

→ → → → → → → → → → → →
Turn to page 55.

You walk over and take one of the leaflets. It features a caricature of the leader of the provisional government, Kerensky, with his arm outstretched, ordering a column of ragged soldiers into the mouth of a huge skull. The caption underneath reads, *Kerensky with his stupid operatic poses is sending the Russian people to their deaths, and for what? For his own wealth and power!*

"Excuse me. Can you tell me where the Bearpit Café is?" you ask.

"The Bearpit? But of course. I practically live there," the young man says. "Hold on a moment."

He gives his last leaflet to the officer, who is still standing there, looking somewhat dazed.

"My name is Sergei," the young man says, introducing himself to you. "I notice that you have an English accent. You are English?"

"No, I'm American," you say. "My name is Indiana Jones."

"What brings you to Petrograd?"

"I'm an agricultural consultant, and—"

"You look more like a spy to me," Sergei interrupts. "The American capitalists are afraid of our revolution, are they?"

→ → → → → → → → → → → → →
Go on to the next page.

"I don't know anything about that," you say.

"Well, if you are a spy, I won't tell," Sergei says. "Half my friends are spies for somebody—the government, the czarists, the Germans, the Poles, the Czechs, even the Japanese. Some are double agents, spying for one side one day, the other side the next."

Sergei guides you off the boulevard and into the darkened side streets. Petrograd is far enough to the north so that the midsummer twilight lasts well into the night. You can see piles of torn newspapers scattered along the street. The walls of most of the buildings are covered with posters, some old and peeling off, some freshly posted. The air smells of printer's ink.

A short time later, Sergei leads you across a broad square ablaze with shop windows and electric signs. The many art gallery windows are filled with abstract paintings in the startling new style that you've heard about. Well-dressed crowds are lined up outside theaters, and you see several outdoor cafés filled to capacity.

Finally you arrive at the Bearpit. There's a large crowd outside, mostly students, waiting to get in. Sergei pulls you behind him as he pushes his way through the crowd to the front door. Several heavyset bearded bouncers wearing red armbands wave Sergei—and you—through the door of the café. Fortunately, Sergei seems to have a certain amount of influence.

The inside of the Bearpit is throbbing with music from a small band and packed with people. White-shirted waiters run back and forth from a wooden counter along one wall, ferrying trays of glasses of vodka and tea and plates of small sausages. The air is filled with cigarette smoke. You scan the crowd, looking for Olaf, but you don't see him.

Sergei guides you to a table where a young woman and an undernourished young man in a priest's cassock greet him enthusiastically.

"This is Rosa. She's a medical student. And this is Dmitri, who as you can see is studying for the priesthood," Sergei says, introducing them. Turning to you, he gestures to his friends. "This is Indiana Jones, my new friend from America. You see, the whole world is interested in our revolution."

"I just finished reading *War and the Future*, by your writer H. G. Wells," Rosa says.

"Wells, I believe, is a British writer," you say. "But an interesting one nonetheless."

Rosa giggles. "Oops," she says. "Well, I *did* read it in English."

"H. G. Wells, Bernard Shaw, and our own Maxim Gorky all think they know how to create a paradise on earth like they can in their books. It's just not possible," Dmitri says.

"Who says it isn't possible, Dmitri? Anything's possible. Now that the czar is gone, *we* can decide the future," Sergei says.

"Paradise is in heaven," Dmitri says. "Trying to create one on earth always backfires. It can only lead to more suffering."

→ → → → → → → → → → → →
Go on to the next page.

"Spoken like a true pessimist. I admire that, I really do," Sergei says, slapping Dmitri gently on the back.

"Things are bound to get better," Rosa says. "But I'll have to admit they couldn't be any worse right now. Children are dying in the hospital for lack of medicine—it's all needed at the front. The war is ruining us like it's ruining everything else in Russia."

"Good! Good!" Sergei exclaims. "Now you're beginning to sound like a true Bolshevik."

"You don't have to be a Bolshevik to be against the war. Everyone hates the war," Rosa says. "As soon as the provisional government holds the elections, I'm sure—"

"Elections!" Sergei interrupts. "You really think the government is going to hold elections? You've got to be—"

A disturbance in the far corner of the café distracts Sergei's attention. A wild-haired and wild-bearded figure is shouting and waving his arms. Another person, whom you recognize as Olaf, is trying to calm him down.

"That's just Boris, our wild anarchist in residence," Rosa says. "He gets into a fistfight with someone every night."

"And gets thrown out every night," Sergei says. "But they always let him back in the next day. It livens things up around here."

You see a man jump up and shake his fist at Boris. Suddenly you realize that it's another friend of yours—John Reed.

"I know them!" you exclaim.

"You know Boris?" Rosa says.

"No, the other two. One of them is my friend Olaf. The other is the writer John Reed. We rode together with Pancho Villa back in Mexico."

"Pancho Villa. Isn't he the revolutionary who invaded the United States?" Sergei asks.

"It wasn't exactly an invasion. More like a small raid. I was there," you say.

Rosa looks at you skeptically.

"Look, if Indy here claims to have been there, then we must believe our friend," Sergei says. "But let's just see what this John Reed has to say about it."

You, Sergei, and Rosa get up and head toward the argument. Dmitri elects to stay behind.

As you arrive at their table, Reed and Boris look as if they are about to trade blows.

"All government is evil! All government is corrupt!" Boris shouts. "I say kill *all* the politicians. Let the streets run with their blood." He picks up a bottle of vodka from the table and takes a long swig.

"I think the revolutionaries should take over the government and—" Reed starts.

→ → → → → → → → → → → →
Go on to the next page.

Boris turns to the crowd in the café. "Don't write us anarchists off too soon, you bourgeois cretins," he interrupts. "Government evil... evil government..." His voice trails off as he falls sideways. Reed catches him and eases him gently into a chair.

"I think he had one too many vodkas," Olaf says.

"Funny," Reed says. "I agree with Boris in a way, but not about the bloodshed and—"

Reed looks at you. He stares in amazement for a few seconds, then grabs your hand. "Indy, my friend, fancy seeing you here. Hey," he announces to Olaf, "we rode together with Pancho Villa... in Mexico!"

Rosa looks at you, impressed. "So you weren't kidding," she says.

Olaf also looks surprised. "This is the one I told you about—the one who came with me from Stockholm," he tells Reed.

"Why didn't you tell me it was my friend from Mexico?" Reed says.

"Honestly, I didn't know that you two knew each other," Olaf says.

"Well, I'm really glad you're here," Reed tells you. "For color and grandeur, the revolution in Russia makes Mexico look pale. We're at the center of one of the great turning points of history."

→ → → → → → → → → → → → →
Go on to the next page.

"I think you're right," you say.

"Viva la revolución!" Reed shouts in Spanish.

"Long live the revolution," you repeat, getting into the spirit of things.

You notice a young woman waving from across the café. She is trying to work her way through the crowd and over to your group. She finally makes it, out of breath. Sergei introduces you to her. Her name is Irena.

"I just came from the speech given by Lenin at the Keshinskiya Palace," Irena says.

"I'll bet he got the crowd all worked up and ready to march on the government right now," Sergei says excitedly.

"No," Irena says. "He told them that the time is not ripe and that they should be patient."

"Patient! He's got to be joking," Sergei says. "Now is the time to act. The provisional government is crumbling, the soldiers of the Petrograd garrison and the sailors at the Kronstadt Naval Base are with us. Only a few old cossacks support the government."

"Don't be too sure," Reed says. "Lenin keeps shouting 'All power to the Soviets,' but the Soviets are still in the hands of the Mensheviks and don't really support the Bolsheviks as yet. And remember, even if you Bolsheviks seize power here in Petrograd, the rest of the country may not necessarily go along with it."

"Bolsheviks, Mensheviks, Soviets—I'm getting a little confused by all this," you say.

"It's very simple," Rosa says. "The term 'Bolshevik' comes from a Russian word meaning 'more' or 'majority,' even though the Bolsheviks are really in the minority. Menshevik means 'minority,' even though they form the majority."

"Well, that certainly makes everything clear," you say jokingly.

"The Soviets are councils set up by the workers, the soldiers, the sailors, and the peasants all across the country. Most of them now have representatives here in Petrograd," Irena says.

"Hold on," Reed says. "That's enough political education for now. I've got to get Boris home. Help me get him to the door. Rosa and Irena, go out and see if you can borrow a wheelbarrow somewhere."

→ → → → → → → → → → → →
Go on to the next page.

Ten minutes later, you, Reed, Sergei, and Olaf exit the Bearpit carrying Boris's inert body. Together you deposit him in the large wheelbarrow that Rosa and Irena have found. The crowd outside lets out a cheer at yet another of Reed's practical jokes.

"I must get back to the hospital," Rosa says. "I'll be at the apartment later."

"I must be going, too," Olaf says.

"Sergei and I are going to the apartment now," Irena tells you. "Why don't you come with us? Maybe we can scrape up some food."

"And discuss a few things," Sergei adds.

"I still have to get Boris home," Reed says. "If the soldiers catch him, they'll beat him up again. Just his appearance seems to get them mad."

"They're liberal, but they have a dim view of anarchists," Irena says.

"Why don't you come with me?" Reed asks you. "After I deposit Boris, I'm going to the studio of an artist friend of mine, a painter named Kasimir Malevich. He is turning out some of the best posters of the revolution. He's even creating a revolution of his own in art."

→ → → → → → → → → → → → →
Go on to the next page.

You'd like to talk more with Sergei and Irena.
On the other hand, you'd also like to talk to Reed
and see this new kind of art he's talking about.
As your friends say their good-byes, you try to
decide what you're going to do.

→ → → → → → → → → → → → →

If you decide to go with Sergei and Irena,
turn to page 79.

If you decide to go with Reed,
turn to page 97.

You decide to go to the steelworks. You rush up to the guard at the front door of the embassy. "Do we have any cars, trucks, horses—anything? I need to get somewhere fast."

The guard looks somewhat startled, but he knows that you are a member of the staff. "There's a truck we use for picking up supplies. It's usually parked on the other side of the building, at the service entrance. But I don't know if—"

→ → → → → → → → → → → →

Go on to the next page.

You are already running to the corner and around the block. Up ahead you see the truck. The driver is at the wheel, asleep. You gently shake him awake and show him your identification. "I'm on a special mission for the ambassador—it's very important. Do you know where the Putilov Steelworks are?"

"Sure," he says. "My brother works there. I take him to work sometimes."

"Then let's go. I need to get there right away."

"I think it's very dangerous to go there right now. The Bolsheviks have the place closed down and—"

"Is your brother there now?"

"I'm not sure. He may be."

"Then, if you want to save his life, you'd better take me there fast," you say, climbing into the seat next to him.

$\rightarrow$ $\rightarrow$ $\rightarrow$ $\rightarrow$ $\rightarrow$ $\rightarrow$ $\rightarrow$ $\rightarrow$ $\rightarrow$ $\rightarrow$ $\rightarrow$ $\rightarrow$

Turn to page 80.

You cross a wide, open square, then proceed down a side street to the Neva. It's true—you've never seen anything like the buildings along the river. Their facades are lavishly decorated with gilded ornaments and tipped with fantastic cupolas and pinnacles. Sergei and Irena stop in front of a huge colonnaded entranceway.

"In here," Irena says. "Don't you just love it?"

Inside is a high-ceilinged foyer with a broad marble staircase leading upward. An enormous crystal chandelier hangs from the center of the ceiling.

At the top of the stairway, your new friends lead you down a long, wide hallway to the door of their "apartment." Inside it looks like a nomad's encampment.

"Let's see if we can find some food," Irena says, walking over to a small coal stove, its stovepipe sticking out the window next to it.

"I think we have some cabbage left, and a potato. I'll peel it," she adds.

"Just cut it up and put it in the pot with the cabbage," Sergei says. "That way we won't waste the peel."

"You could just make some soup with it," you say.

"Good idea," Irena says. "Just keep Sergei out of my way until it's done."

→ → → → → → → → → → → →

Go on to the next page.

"All right, while you're doing that, I'm going to finish this," Sergei says, walking over to a banner tacked up on one of the walls. You walk over to it with him.

"Tell me more about yourself," Sergei says, as he picks up a brush from the floor.

"I'm here as an agricultural consultant—for the French embassy," you say, trying to keep a straight face.

"That's an interesting combination," Sergei says, adding a few words in Russian to the banner. "I didn't know the French were so interested in our agriculture. They seem to be more interested in keeping Russia in the war against Germany. The Russian workers, of course, want peace."

"I think everyone wants peace," you say.

Sergei laughs. "Oh, sure they do," he says sarcastically. "Don't you know that the capitalistic system can't exist without war? The capitalists need the huge profits they make by producing weapons so that they can live in luxury while they use the masses as slave laborers and cannon fodder. You can ask your friend John Reed about that."

"I would like to see a better world for everybody," you say.

"I believe you," Sergei says, dipping the brush in a can of red paint and adding another letter to his banner. "Just be careful that the reactionaries do not use you as their tool."

"I'll be careful," you say.

"Oh, by the way," Sergei says casually, "since you're such an agricultural expert, what do you think about the collectivization of agriculture? If all the farmers worked together in collectives, don't you think production would be much more efficient?"

"Well...I think...that might work," you stumble along.

"When the revolution is complete, Irena and I are moving to the country and starting an agricultural commune. Maybe you could come with us and help set it up. You could help us decide which crops would be the most—"

"The soup is ready," Irena calls out from the other side of the room.

You give a sigh of relief at not having to answer any more of Sergei's questions about agriculture for the moment. You are tempted to just tell them the truth. But you guess that they've already figured it out anyway.

"Where are you staying?" Irena asks, as she hands you a bowl of steaming soup.

"I'm not staying anywhere. I mean, I just arrived in the city, and I'm not settled yet," you say.

→ → → → → → → → → → → →
Go on to the next page.

"Why don't you move into this building? There's an empty room across the corridor," Irena says. "I even think Princess What's-her-name left some furniture in there."

"And your windows will look out over the Neva River," Sergei says.

"I'd like that," you say. "I'll bring my stuff over later. That way I can move in on my birthday."

Irena jumps up, almost spilling her soup. "Today is your birthday!" she exclaims. "I think that calls for a celebration."

"But you don't even really know me yet," you say.

"You're a friend of Olaf and John Reed," Irena says. "That's enough for us."

"In times such as these, each day is a lifetime," Sergei says. "We must at least share a drink with you and your friends at the Bearpit."

"That would be fine," you say. "But right now, I'd better get back to my job."

"Your agricultural duties call," Sergei says.

"Seriously, Sergei, thanks for everything," you say. "It's great to find such good friends."

You shake their hands good-bye, then head back to the embassy.

The French embassy is only a twenty-minute walk from the Red Palace. You make a few wrong turns at first, but you have no trouble finding it. You go in the front door and start down the hallway leading to the basement stairs. There you meet your associate, Brossard, coming up.

"Ah, Captain Defense, it's a good thing you're back," he says. "There's a staff meeting with the ambassador himself right now. Come, we'd better hurry."

You follow Brossard up the impressive grand stairway of the embassy and then down a paneled hallway to the main conference room next to the ambassador's office. Inside, members of the embassy staff are seated at a large, gleaming table. You follow Brossard to a row of chairs on the left-hand side of the table and sit down. Brossard places a thick sheaf of papers on the table in front of him.

"I've got all the facts right here," he says, patting the pile of papers. "I'm ready for anything the ambassador asks me."

"All right, suppose he asks you for the date and time of the Bolsheviks' attempt to take over," you say.

"Well, of course I don't know the exact date as yet. But I'll know it soon. Maybe *you* can tell me?"

"Why should I tell you?" you say.

"Because that's supposed to be your job. We're supposed to be working together."

→ → → → → → → → → → → →
Go on to the next page.

Brossard's voice rises as he says this, and several members of the staff look over at him sternly.

"Don't worry, Brossard. I'll tell you as soon as I find out," you say.

Everyone rises as the ambassador, in full ceremonial uniform, enters the room. Laurentine comes in right behind him. The ambassador sits down at the head of the conference table, then signals for everyone to be seated.

"I've just come from a meeting with Kerensky and the members of the provisional government," the ambassador says. "I must tell you— in the strictest confidence—that I seriously doubt whether they can hold on to their power until the elections."

"Things have grown more and more volatile ever since Lenin returned from exile. The next three months are crucial," Laurentine adds.

"I believe there could be a Bolshevik insurrection any time in the next two weeks," the ambassador goes on. "The provisional government is desperate for any information. I expect all of you to work with the utmost diligence."

→ → → → → → → → → → → →

Go on to the next page.

"Remember, if the Bolsheviks come to power and Russia pulls out of the war, millions of German troops will be free to come over to the battlefields of France and overrun us. It's as simple as that," Laurentine says.

"I might add that there will probably be a promotion in this for whoever provides the information we need. And a more attractive assignment. That is all I have to say. This meeting stands adjourned," the ambassador says.

You and Brossard head back down the main staircase.

"Look," you say. "I don't want to make this a contest between us, despite what the ambassador said back there."

"Thanks," Brossard says. "I just want to get out of the basement and do something above ground."

"Why aren't you doing just that?" you say. "I think you just need to assert yourself a little more."

"The thing is that I'm nearsighted and not very strong physically. Laurentine won't take me seriously as a field operative."

"Brossard, you're just the type that makes the *best* field operative. Those like me tend to stick out like sore thumbs. Do you know that since I've been in Petrograd, not one person has taken my cover seriously? You could pass for an agricultural consultant much better than I can."

"You really think so?" Brossard says.

"I do," you say. "Go back to your file cabinets bravely—and remember, you won't be there much longer."

Brossard goes down the hall with a smile on his face. You're not really sure what you meant by that last statement, but at least it made him happy, you figure.

← ← ← ← ← ← ← ← ← ← ← ←
Turn to page 25.

You decide to go to the Bearpit Café. As you leave the embassy, a brilliant red sunset lights up the sky to the west. It somehow seems very symbolic.

You walk over to a street corner, hoping to find someone to ask directions to the café. You see a streetcar coming up the avenue, its side plastered with revolutionary posters. It's followed by a column of what appear to be workers. They're wearing overalls, and their shirtsleeves are rolled up. They are also carrying broad banners that read ALL POWER TO THE SOVIETS and DOWN WITH THE WAR.

You stand beside several well-dressed people and a young officer festooned with gold braid. An elaborately decorated sword hangs at his side. You watch as the little parade goes by.

You are about to continue up the avenue when you see a young man about your own age walking along behind the marchers and handing out leaflets.

← ← ← ← ← ← ← ← ← ← ←
Turn to page 27.

"There! Isn't that beautiful?" Rosa asks.

"Yes, it's fine," you say. "Thanks for showing it to me. Well, I've got to—"

"There are hundreds of bridges in Petrograd, all different, and yet all somehow . . . alike."

"I guess so," you say.

Rosa starts off again. "If we go back this way, we'll pass a bridge with four gilded griffins— you know, those mythical animals that have the head and wings of an eagle and the body of a lion. There it is up ahead. Aren't the griffins beautiful?" she says. "Come, there's another bridge down this way."

After another few blocks, Rosa guides you across it. "Do you like those?" she says, pointing up at the turrets that flank the bridge.

"Sure. Is this the way to the apartment?" you ask.

"Sort of. If we go just another few blocks, there's another bridge with the most amazing cast iron railings."

"I like your bridges, but my feet are really getting tired," you say.

Rosa glances at her watch. "Yes," she says. "It is getting late, we'd better—oh no!"

"What's the matter?"

"I must have dropped my small purse. I know I had it with me just before we looked at the bridge with the griffins."

→ → → → → → → → → → → → →

Go on to the next page.

"All the way back there?" you ask.

"I think so," she says. "It won't take all that long to go back and look."

Just before you get to the griffin bridge, Rosa casually reaches into one of her pockets. "Well, look at that," she says, pulling out her purse. "I must have stuck it in there and forgotten about it."

"*Now* can we go to the apartment?" you ask.

"Sure," she says. "We'd better hurry. It's getting late."

The Red Palace apartment complex seems strangely quiet as you and Rosa go up the front stairway. In the hallway, all the doors are closed. Rosa knocks on the door to Irena and Sergei's apartment and steps back. As the door opens, you stare inside in amazement. The room is packed with people, including your friends Olaf, John Reed, Sergei, Dmitri, Irena, and Boris, as well as dozens of others from the Bearpit.

"Surprise! Happy Birthday!" they all shout.

Homemade decorations have been draped around the room, and there is a table in the center with refreshments.

"Fooled you, didn't I?" Rosa says.

Soon the party is in full swing. Several of the musicians from the Bearpit are there, and people start dancing.

→ → → → → → → → → → → →
Go on to the next page.

"How about cutting your cake?" Sergei says. "We're all hungry."

"A cake!" you say.

Irena proudly brings out a medium-sized round cake covered with white icing and puts it on the table. It has a single lit candle stuck in the middle. "This is a true revolutionary cake—more ingenuity than raisins," she says.

Sergei hands you a knife, and everyone crowds around you as you prepare to cut the cake.

"Now this is typical," Boris says in a joking tone. "If there's a cake—who gets to divide it? The capitalist."

"The person whose birthday it is gets to cut the cake," Dmitri says.

Sergei laughs and takes the knife back. "That's how things used to be, Dmitri. Everything used to depend on birth," he says.

Irena snatches the knife from Sergei and cuts a large slice. "If you were born a noble, you got this much. If you were born a peasant or a worker, you got *this* much," she says, cutting a much smaller slice.

"That's the way feudalism is," Sergei says. "Now that the czar's gone, we're through with it."

You grab the knife back. "Whereas, if you wisely decide to become capitalists, the person who bakes the cake gets the biggest slice—all because she's smart and ingenious," you join in.

John Reed takes the knife. "But the peasants who grew the wheat, and the workers who milled it and mixed it with the other ingredients, used to get only tiny bits of the cake. So the way to achieve justice is through socialism. The smart capitalist can bake the cake, but the government, in this case me, makes sure all the workers get a fair share," he says, as he makes equal marks in the icing.

"It won't work, John," Irena says. "The capitalists are too smart for that. You try getting the cake out of their hands, and it falls to pieces. No, the *people* must bake the cake and the *state* divide it up, so that everyone gets a fair share according to their needs. This is what true communism is all about." Then she takes the knife and divides the cake into equal pieces.

→ → → → → → → → → → → → →

Go on to the next page.

Suddenly Boris grabs several of the pieces and crams them into his mouth. "And this is what anarchism is all about."

Sergei, Olaf, and Reed grab him and drag him away from the cake, laughing.

You, at least, get the next piece.

While this has been going on, word has gotten around about the affair here at the Red Palace. It has expanded into more than just your birthday party. The hallway outside has filled up with people having a good time. The crowd extends all the way down the main staircase and out onto the street. The party goes on for hours, through the "white night" of midsummer Petrograd.

Finally you sneak across the hallway and into your room, locking the door from the inside. As you lie down on your new bed, you can still hear music and laughter throughout the building.

You wake up about noon the next day. You get dressed and go out into the hallway, threading your way around the bodies sleeping off too much vodka from the night before. Then you take a long walk along the river, thinking about your new friends and trying to sort things out. You certainly have more in common with them than with the stuffy bureaucrats at the embassy.

The weather is hot, but the sky is clear, and there's a nice breeze coming off the river. I really should take the rest of the day off, you think.

On the other hand, you do have a responsibility to the people you're working for. Maybe if you report in at the embassy, they'll send you right out again anyway.

← ← ← ← ← ← ← ← ← ← ← ←
*If you decide to take the rest of the day off,
turn to page 5.*

→ → → → → → → → → → → →
*If you decide to report to the embassy,
turn to page 105.*

"**I** think I'll go by way of Finland," you say. "Now how exactly would I do that?"

"Very simple, *mon ami*," Charles explains. "You take the train across the Pyrenees Mountains to France. From there you take a boat to Sweden, where you cross over into Finland— and from there to Russia."

"Somehow it doesn't sound all that simple," you say.

"Inside here you will find all the details," Charles says, handing you an envelope. "Your cover story will be that you are an agricultural advisor attached to the French embassy."

"But I don't know anything about agriculture," you say.

"No matter, no one will believe that you are really an agricultural advisor, anyway."

You shake hands with Charles and say goodbye. On your way back to your hotel, you stop as you pass by several other buildings designed by Gaudi, the eccentric architect of Barcelona. They are huge structures, built with strange, twisting shapes and completely covered with mosaics of brightly colored tile.

← ← ← ← ← ← ← ← ← ← ← ←
Turn to page 7.

"Then why all the activity?" you say. "I see piles of leaflets on the table over there calling for the overthrow of the provisional government. You're polishing up your speech, and you have your banner ready to go."

"It's important that we keep working for the revolution and building up our organization," Sergei says. "But the time is not right to try to overthrow the government."

"Why not?" you ask.

"First, try this cup of tea, and here's a slice of good Russian black bread," Irena says.

"Thanks, that tastes good," you say. "But how about 'why not?'"

"For one thing," Irena says, "our leader, Lenin, is on his way to Finland."

"Why so? You'd think he'd want to stay on top of the action here."

"The man is exhausted. He's worn out, and he's going to Finland to recuperate. He knows that this is not the right time to move."

"It seems to me that you and the Bolsheviks could take Petrograd right now," you say.

"We'd hold it about a week before being thrown out. The simple fact is that not enough people support us yet. In a few months we'll be ready, but not today, not just yet," Irena says.

→ → → → → → → → → → → →

Go on to the next page.

"If you tell the French that the Bolshevik Revolution is going to happen before then, you'll end up with egg on your face. Believe me, this is not the time," Sergei says.

"I appreciate your telling me that," you say, getting up to leave. "I'm going to get a good night's sleep tonight. Thanks for the birthday party last night. It was the best one I ever had. And watch out for yourselves. Whether the Bolshevik Revolution is starting or not, the reactionaries are still vicious and bloodthirsty."

"Tell us about it," Sergei says.

The next day you get up early and stroll in a leisurely manner to the embassy. When you get there, no one is in the basement room. You decide to look into Laurentine's office. Unexpectedly, you find Laurentine, Brossard, and the ambassador, grouped around Laurentine's desk.

"I'm sorry," you say. "I didn't mean to—"

"As a matter of fact," Laurentine says, "we were looking for you. We've been working all night. Sit down over here. The ambassador was just telling us about the latest communication from Paris."

"My superiors in Paris are demanding a full report today. We must be able to tell them what is happening here," the ambassador says.

→ → → → → → → → → → → → →
Go on to the next page.

"Sir," Brossard speaks up, "I've been working on it all night. I believe the Bolshevik uprising will begin sometime in the next twenty-four hours, Ambassador."

"Really? Do you have any proof of that?" the ambassador says.

Brossard rustles through his papers and pulls out a list. "Proof one, the latest offensive against the Germans is failing, and more and more soldiers are deserting from the front. Proof two, regiments stationed in Petrograd itself are refusing to go to the front and are thus available for insurrection here. The most dangerous are the Machine Gun Regiment and the Kronstadt sailors. Proof three, in the next twenty-four hours—"

"For Pete's sake, Brossard, all this is meaningless," you say, interrupting. "There's not going to be an uprising right now."

"Let's let Captain Brossard finish his presentation," Laurentine says. "You'll get your chance to speak."

The ambassador gives you a very annoyed look.

"As I was saying," Brossard goes on, "in the next twenty-four hours, there are more protest meetings scheduled than at any time since the czar fell. I believe the insurrection will start with a march by the Putilov steelworkers on the Keshinskiya Palace sometime today."

"Very good reasoning, Brossard," the ambassador says.

"Now what's your problem with this, Captain Defense?" Laurentine asks.

"The timing is wrong, all wrong," you say. "The Bolsheviks haven't got enough support with either the workers or the soldiers, certainly not with the peasants across the country. They know that they could capture Petrograd, but they also know they couldn't hold it."

"There's a lot of truth in that, Ambassador," Laurentine says. "The Bolsheviks are dangerous, but they're also cautious."

"I just don't believe it," Brossard says. "Lenin has been whipping up his followers. He must know that if the Bolsheviks storm the palace now, there's precious little to stop them."

"I'm glad you brought up Lenin, Brossard," you say. "Just where do you think he is right now?"

"Out giving speeches, I'm sure," Brossard says.

"If you check, I think you'll find that Lenin is in Finland. Hardly a place from which to mount a coup d'état in Petrograd."

→ → → → → → → → → → → →

Go on to the next page.

"I don't believe it," Brossard says.

"I think we can settle this matter very quickly," Laurentine says. "I've just been handed a report on Lenin's whereabouts as of a few hours ago."

Laurentine tears open the sealed envelope and takes out a document. He scans it and looks up, a surprised expression on his face.

"Captain Defense is quite correct, Ambassador. Lenin crossed the Finnish border this morning. He's reported to be suffering from extreme nervous exhaustion."

"It seems I've misjudged you, Captain Defense," the ambassador says. "I compliment you on your good intelligence work. Interesting thinking, Brossard, but perhaps you let your enthusiasm run away with you."

"I'm sorry, sir," Brossard says.

The ambassador gets up from his chair. "I think I have what I need to report to my superiors. It looks as though the Bolshevik uprising is not yet upon us. Good day."

The ambassador goes out with Laurentine following behind.

"You rat, you filthy—" Brossard starts.

"Look, I'm sorry, Brossard," you say. "I didn't get a chance to talk to you ahead of time, and you just went on and on with your 'proof one, proof two,' and all that."

"I guess you're right," Brossard says. "I'm sure you would have told me if you had had the chance. I'm sorry I got so upset."

"All water under the bridge, Brossard," you say. "Come, let's go down to our basement cave and pretend we're working for a while."

→ → → → → → → → → → → →
Go on to the next page.

Later, down in the basement, you sit with your feet up on your desk—which you finally clear off with the help of Brossard. While you look through a French magazine you happened to find in your desk drawer, Brossard, still the workhorse, sits hunched over his desk, studying reports.

"You're a good deskman, Brossard," you say. "But I hope to see you out in the real world soon."

"After the discrediting you gave me before," Brossard says, "I'll be lucky to have any kind of job at all with this outfit."

Suddenly Laurentine bursts into the room. "Captain Defense, Captain Brossard, report at once to the crisis room above the ambassador's office," he shouts.

"Crisis room?" Brossard says. "I didn't know we had one."

"We do now," Laurentine says. "The Bolshevik uprising began an hour ago."

Brossard gives you a penetrating look. The two of you follow Laurentine from the basement and up the grand staircase, two steps at a time.

"Maybe you're not as smart as you think you are," Brossard says, already out of breath.

The "crisis room" is filled with tables, telephones, and maps. People are running in and out. The ambassador gives you a cold look as you approach one of the tables and sit down, still bewildered.

→ → → → → → → → → → → → →

Go on to the next page.

"Captain Defense, take one of the phones there on the table. Brossard, you come over here with me," Laurentine says.

Other members of the staff are manning several more phones. One of them calls out to the ambassador, "The Machine Gun Regiment has taken over the Finland Station."

Your phone rings. You pick it up and put the speaker to your ear. A voice somewhere on the other end says, "There are Bolshevik armored cars at the intersection of Shpalernaya Street and the Liteiny Prospect." You repeat this for Laurentine, who is putting pins on a large map of Petrograd on the wall. Several other men call out different locations.

"That does it," Laurentine says. "There are Bolshevik armored cars at all the major intersections."

"They've blocked all the bridges over the Neva also," someone else calls out. "And the Kronstadt sailors are heading for the city—ten thousand of them."

→ → → → → → → → → → → →
Go on to the next page.

Someone runs in with a dispatch and hands it to Laurentine. "Captain Defense, you should be interested in this," he says. "Lenin has returned from Finland and is addressing a massive crowd in front of Bolshevik Headquarters."

"Come on," you say. "Don't rub it in."

You wonder about Sergei and Irena. Did they really try to sell you a bill of goods? Or were they in the dark themselves? The leaders don't always tell their followers everything.

You'll have to sort all that out later. Right now you're too busy to think about it.

The work goes on for several hours. Later, the ambassador, now in his shirtsleeves and looking weary, sits at one of the tables drinking black coffee. Laurentine sits down beside him. "Well, it looks as though a few hours from now you'll be the first French ambassador to Bolshevik Russia," he says.

"A few hours from now I won't be an ambassador at all. France will never recognize a Bolshevik Russia."

A courier comes in and hands Laurentine an envelope. "Here's the text of the speech Lenin gave an hour ago to the Kronstadt sailors," he says.

Laurentine puts the envelope on the table.

"Aren't you going to open and read it?" you ask.

"I already know what it says," Laurentine replies. "Down with Kerensky, down with the provisional government, down with the war, and so forth. You can read it if you like. Just don't tell me about it."

You take the envelope and open it. You start reading, and then start laughing.

"I don't think it's so funny," Laurentine says. "Or maybe the strain has finally gotten to you and your mind is going."

"You want to know what Lenin told the sailors?" you say.

"No, I don't want to hear."

"He told them to go home."

"What! Let me see that." Laurentine snatches the report out of your hand and reads it out loud.

"'Comrades, you must excuse me,'" Laurentine reads, "'I've been ill. The circumstances of the moment demand that we be patient. The time is not right for insurrection. Please go home and wait until you are called upon.'"

"Fighting talk," you say.

"Are they listening to him, though?" the ambassador asks.

"I'll find out, sir," Brossard says. He makes a call on one of the telephones. "The Bolshevik leaders are trying to restrain their followers, but they're not having much success," he says.

"The people may be taking the initiative themselves," Laurentine says.

→ → → → → → → → → → → →

Go on to the next page.

"Here's another report," Brossard says. "The cossacks have decided to back the government. They've posted snipers on the rooftops overlooking the main streets, particularly the routes from the Putilov Steelworks."

The steelworks! You remember that Sergei and Irena are going there. They're in big trouble, you realize.

"Excuse me," you say. "I'm going out to get some information firsthand."

"All right, but—" Laurentine starts.

You never hear the end of his statement. You are already bounding down the embassy staircase three steps at a time. Sergei and Irena may have tried to trick you—you're still not sure—but you like them a lot even if they did, and you don't want anything to happen to them.

You could rush back to the apartment to see if they've left, or you could go directly to the steelworks. You've got to decide what to do, fast.

→ → → → → → → → → → → →

If you decide to rush back to the apartment, turn to page 103.

← ← ← ← ← ← ← ← ← ← ← ←

If you decide to go to the steelworks, turn to page 41.

Yn decide to go with Sergei and Irena.

"I hope we can get together again," you tell Reed. "We've got a lot to talk about. I've had a few adventures since Mexico."

Reed laughs. "And so have I," he says.

You wave good-bye to Reed as he wheels the now-snoring Boris away down the street. Then you follow Sergei and Irena in the opposite direction. After a short distance, you turn down a broad street lined with large, elaborately decorated buildings. They seem to go on as far as the eye can see.

"This city was certainly built on a huge scale," you say.

"These are just government buildings," Irena says. "Wait until you see the palaces on the Neva River. We're living in one."

"In a palace?" you say.

"Sergei and I, and some of the crowd from the Bearpit have turned one into an apartment complex—unofficially as far as the authorities are concerned. The owners fled the city when the revolution started. We've renamed it the 'Red Palace.'"

← ← ← ← ← ← ← ← ← ← ← ←

Turn to page 45.

The truck takes off with a few explosions from the exhaust, then careens down the cobblestone streets of Petrograd. The pedestrians are used to having the streets mostly to themselves. The driver drives with one hand and keeps the other on the horn to warn them.

After a while, you reach the outskirts of the city. The massive structure of the steelworks looms ahead of you.

After a few more minutes, the truck comes to a screeching stop at the front gate. It's guarded by a line of workers with red armbands.

"If your brother values his life, tell him not to march today with the other workers," you say.

Then you jump out and run up to the gate. There's a huge crowd inside listening to someone speaking.

You see that the speaker is Sergei. Irena is moving through the crowd, handing out pamphlets.

A guard by the gate grabs you as you start to go in. "Only steelworkers are allowed inside," he says.

"But that's my friend there giving a speech. I've come to hear him," you say.

"That's *your* story," the guard says. "Now beat it."

Fortunately, you manage to catch Irena's attention, and you wave to her. She comes over and talks to the guard. "This is a friend of the workers," she says, pulling you through the gate.

"I'm glad you came to join us," Irena says.

"I didn't come to join you, I came to warn you."

There are cheers and applause as Sergei finishes his speech. He then comes over to you and Irena.

He looks at you with some surprise. Then he smiles and grabs you by the arm. "I'm glad you're here," he says. "Our plans have changed. We're ready to take over the government—now! We're marching on the Keshinskiya Palace."

"Don't do it, Sergei," you say. "The cossacks have set up an ambush on the street leading to the palace. The rooftops are crawling with snipers."

"We're not pulling out now," Irena says. "Besides, how do we know you're telling the truth—you haven't told us the whole truth up till now. We know you were really with us to collect information for our enemies."

"Hold on a second, Irena," Sergei says. "We each knew what the other was doing. I didn't care because I know deep down that Indy is really with us. After all, Indy did ride with Pancho Villa."

→ → → → → → → → → → → → →

Go on to the next page.

"Sergei, listen to me," you plead. "I'm telling the truth. I'm an agent for French Intelligence. I know the facts."

"I know that," Sergei says. "Nonetheless, the revolution will either succeed today or it will not succeed today. I will either live today or die. It's no matter. If we fail, it will only be a temporary setback for Bolshevism. Soldiers go into battle because they are like sheep being led to the slaughter. We march because we believe in a cause greater than ourselves. If the revolutionaries in your country had not been willing to die, yours would still be a colony of England."

"I hear you, Sergei, but there must be another way."

"Sorry, my friend, but there is no other way."

Suddenly the gates of the steel mill open, and the crowd surges out. Sergei and Irena quickly unfurl their banner and run up to the front of the marching column, each holding a supporting pole with the banner stretched out between. You march along beside them. A great chorus goes up from the workers behind you as they sing a new anthem:

Arise, the wretched of the Earth
We are nothing—thus let us be everything.

You march into the city, side by side with Sergei, Irena, and the Bolsheviks. Suddenly you hear pops like firecrackers from the rooftops. People start falling to the ground all around you. There are screams as some members of the crowd scatter, dashing for cover in the doorways of the buildings along the street. Others, heads held high and fists upraised, keep marching.

Sergei suddenly gasps and grabs his chest, blood flowing out between his fingers. He drops his end of the banner and sinks to his knees. Irena drops hers and runs over to him. Others pick up the banner and keep marching, even though their comrades are falling around them.

With bullets pinging on the pavement around you, you and Irena manage to get Sergei up off the street and into a protected doorway. Irena takes off her coat and puts it behind his head. "Don't die, Sergei, please don't die," she sobs.

Sergei reaches out and grabs your hand with one of his and Irena's with the other. "So long, friend," he says to you. "And Irena, I always—"

His eyes widen in a sudden spasm of pain, and then his head rolls lifelessly to one side. You reach over and close his eyes.

You find out later that four hundred people died in the attempted coup. Lenin was forced to flee, and the Bolsheviks were smashed for the moment. By October it would be a different story, and the Bolsheviks would come to power—and remain in power for a long time. Despite the evil empire that the Bolsheviks would establish, you will never be able to forget the heroism of your friends.

The End

"**I** think I'll go by way of Serbia, Greece, and Romania," you say.

"Good," Charles says. "I'll arrange for you to leave from the port of Barcelona tonight."

You go back to your hotel and pack a small bag. Just after dark, you meet Charles on a dock in the harbor. He leads you to a rusting hulk of a freighter.

"I know this ship does not look like much, but it will get you there," Charles says.

You say good-bye to Charles and go aboard. At midnight, the rusty freighter sets sail. Your cabin is tiny, with one narrow bunk. It seems kind of cozy. The bunk is comfortable enough.

You wake to a brilliant Mediterranean sunrise that you watch through the porthole of your cabin. You go out on deck and stretch.

"The *Hellas* may not look like much, but she is a good ship—and fast," someone behind you says in English. It's the ship's engineer. "In a few days we will be in Salonika, our home port in Greece. We are loaded with ammunition for the Serbs. We could go puff! before that, but I do not think so." Then he goes off down the deck.

The Mediterranean is calm all the way to Greece, the ship doesn't blow up, and the food is not bad.

Four days later, the ship docks in Salonika, a city of sparkling white buildings with crenelated walls, domes, and minarets stretching above the harbor.

A Greek working for French Intelligence meets you at the dock. "My name is Nikos," he says, introducing himself. "I am to go with you on the train through Serbia."

"How *is* Serbia doing these days?" you ask. "I've heard some rumors that—"

"We call it the 'Land of Death,'" Nikos says. "The Austrians are pulverizing the cities and towns with their long-range artillery. But this is just a minor annoyance for the Serbs."

"A minor annoyance?" you say.

"The real problem is that smallpox, cholera, plague, and typhus are killing off the people there like flies," Nikos says. "But do not worry, American. We will survive."

Later, you take the train with Nikos. It soon crosses the border into Serbia, and you begin to see a distinct change in the countryside. Most of the houses have been burned, and any walls left standing have been battered by gunfire. There are almost no people to be seen, though occasionally an unshaven Serbian soldier in rags waves at the train. Black flags warning of cholera are flapping everywhere.

"Not a pretty picture," Nikos says.

"Horrible!" you say.

→ → → → → → → → → → → → →
Go on to the next page.

"Well, the Serbs brought this war on themselves. A Serbian-inspired terrorist named Princip got it into his head to assassinate the heir to the Austrian throne, and now everyone is paying the price," Nikos says.

Suddenly there's an explosion up ahead. A second later, there is a terrific jolt as your car leaves the tracks. You go flying forward and slam into the partition opposite you. Miraculously, your car has remained upright in the derailment.

"Are you all right?" Nikos, somehow unscathed, asks.

"I don't know," you say. "My arm really hurts."

"Ah, I see. It appears to be broken."

"Ow!" you say. "Broken!"

Nikos helps you out of the train and into a small gully. You look up ahead and see the twisted and smoldering remnants of the dynamited locomotive lying on its side.

Nikos makes a splint for your arm with saplings and strips of cloth torn from your jacket.

"Now what do we do?" you ask.

"We walk," Nikos says.

You and some of the others from the train walk back along the tracks toward the Greek border. Hours later, you get there.

→ → → → → → → → → → → → →
Go on to the next page.

Once over the border, Nikos manages to get a donkey cart, and the two of you ride in relative style to his village.

The village doctor, an old man with a white beard, resets the bone in your arm—it is a compound fracture.

While your arms heals, you stay at Nikos's house. It will take a long time before you're better. His family in the meantime treats you royally, bringing you plates of apples and candied oranges.

At night, there is singing and dancing in the town square. On Sundays, the peasants wear colorful costumes, and often Gypsies arrive and entertain with their wild melodies played on fiddles.

No one in the village seems to know, or care, what is going on in Russia—or even thirty miles away, for that matter.

You know you're probably missing the Bolshevik Revolution, the event of the century, but at least you're having a good vacation. Sometimes you even find yourself wondering if your friend Charles would be mad if he knew how the job he had for you really turned out.

For now, your call for adventure will have to wait.

The End

You decide to cover Lenin's speech at the Keshinskiya Palace. You leave the embassy and, after asking directions from people on the street, find the right streetcar to take you there.

As you get off the streetcar, you join the crowd surging toward the elegant palace.

You enter the palace and find yourself in a palatial ballroom full of elegant pillars and chandeliers. You are just in time to see a short, stocky man with a domelike bald head mount a platform at the far end of the room. It is Vladimir Lenin. A cheer goes up from the tightly packed crowd.

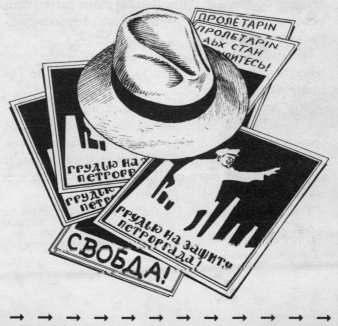

→ → → → → → → → → → → →
Go on to the next page.

After the shouting has died down a bit, Lenin starts speaking. "Comrades! How many of our young men have to die in this war before the capitalists are satisfied? Before they have enough profit from building the guns and the shells? How many—ten thousand? Fifty thousand? A million? Ten million? I say stop the war now!"

Another cheer goes up from the crowd, an even louder one this time.

"Our demands are simple," Lenin continues. "We want peace for the soldiers, bread for the workers, and land for the peasants! Now!"

The crowd starts cheering wildly. Hats are tossed into the air. Some of the hats become caught on the chandeliers overhead.

You feel you have a pretty good idea where Lenin's speech is going. You decide to work your way outside before it's over. You leave the palace. Suddenly you are grabbed by several men and dragged to one of the side buildings. There they take you to a basement room.

"We know you are a capitalist spy from America," one of them says, shining a light in your eyes. "Who are your contacts? Who are your fellow agents?"

→ → → → → → → → → → → →
Go on to the next page.

You give these men your agricultural consultant cover story, but they don't buy it. Finally you try telling them the truth—that you're an agent for French Intelligence. But they don't buy that, either.

They hold you hostage in the basement for several months. Finally, after the Bolsheviks come to power, they release you.

You hike, still dazed, back to the embassy. You go up to the front door where a guard in a plain army uniform is standing. He bars your way as you try to enter.

"But I work here," you protest. "I work for the French embassy."

The guard laughs. "You are a little late," he says. "The French ambassador and his cohorts have left. This is now a barracks for the Red Army."

"Red Army?" you repeat, backing away from the doorway.

You find your way to the Finland Station, the place where you arrived. It is now guarded by well-disciplined Communist soldiers. You manage to purchase a ticket for Sweden with a few rubles that you have secreted away in the lining of your pocket.

→ → → → → → → → → → → →
Go on to the next page.

Once you get to Sweden, you hope you can make contact with your friends Anita and Olaf. You're certainly going to try.

The End

You decide to go with John Reed and meet his friend the painter, Kasimir Malevich. You and Reed take turns pushing the wheelbarrow containing the now-stirring body of Boris. By the time you reach the entrance to his building, Boris is sitting up and giggling.

Reed stops in front and parks the wheelbarrow. "We'll just leave him here," he says. "Boris can be unruly when he's coming out of one of his binges."

You and Reed walk away laughing as Boris begins to thrash his arms around wildly. A few seconds later, the wheelbarrow falls over sideways, dumping Boris in the street.

Several blocks later, Reed leads you into another building and up several flights of stairs. You can smell oil paint and turpentine long before you get to Malevich's studio.

Reed and Kasimir Malevich greet each other with terrific bear hugs. Reed then introduces you. You step back a bit, hoping that the big, hulking painter won't try the same kind of bear hug on you. Fortunately, he doesn't.

"Look at this!" He gestures to you and Reed. *"White on White,* I call it."

For a moment, you see nothing but a seemingly blank canvas. Then you realize that there's a white square painted on a white background.

→ → → → → → → → → → → →

Go on to the next page.

"Suprematism!" Kasimir shouts. "That's what I call suprematism!"

"Do you know about the cubists in Paris—like Picasso?" you ask.

"Cubists! I love them. They have influenced me greatly. But, as you can see, I've gone a step beyond them. I've reduced form to simple geometric shapes."

"I think that's about as far as one can go toward..."

"...toward?" Kasimir says.

"The...ultimate expression of suprematism," Reed says.

"Bravo!" Kasimir roars. "You see, my friend Reed here, he understands me."

Kasimir shows you some more of his paintings with great enthusiasm. Then he shows you the hand-operated printing press he keeps on the other side of the studio. He is printing woodblock posters for the revolutionaries. They are much more representational, mostly showing the workers marching against the capitalists.

"It will take a while before the masses can appreciate my serious work," Kasimir says. "In the meantime, I must do my bit for the political revolution as well as the artistic one."

"We'll let you get back to your work, Kasimir," Reed says.

"It was a pleasure to meet you and see your art," you tell him.

* * *

Back on the street, Reed bids good-bye to you as well. "Thanks for coming to meet Kasimir," he says. "Now I must meet someone on the other side of the city. You won't have any trouble finding your way back to the Bearpit. It's three blocks that way, then two to the right and five to the left. I'll see you again tomorrow."

You say good-night, then head back toward the Bearpit. Halfway there, as you come around a corner, several thugs dash in your direction. One of them hits you on the back of the head, and you black out.

When you come to, you're in a bed in the embassy infirmary. Laurentine is looking down at you. "Looks as though you'll be out of action for a while," he says.

"What? I'm all right," you say, trying to sit up. But it feels as if someone has just hit your head again with a lead pipe.

→ → → → → → → → → → → →

Go on to the next page.

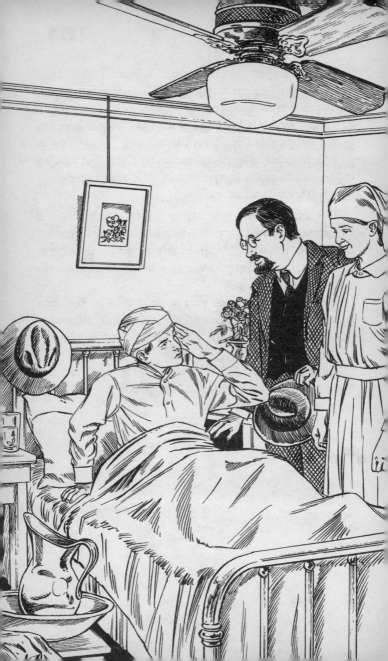

"Just a slight concussion," a nurse standing behind Laurentine says. "We'll need to keep you in bed for a few days."

"Don't worry," Laurentine says. "We'll have a new assignment for you then."

You wonder what he means by that, but you're in too much pain to worry about it now. Besides, you'll find out soon enough.

The End

You decide to go to Sergei and Irena's apartment. When you get there, you find Rosa sitting by the window, crying.

You tell her about the cossacks.

"I know," she says. "I heard about it myself at the hospital. We were warned to stay off the streets. I tried to warn them, but they wouldn't listen."

"Maybe we can still stop Sergei and Irena somehow—before they get to the Keshinskiya Palace," you say.

"I'll try anything," Rosa says.

You and Rosa take the streetcar in the direction of the palace, but it's painfully slow. Finally you abandon it and run.

Then, way up ahead, you see a column of protesters approaching down the avenue. Sergei and Irena are leading it. Seconds later, the cossacks start firing. You see Sergei fall. You and Rosa start running toward him as bullets begin pinging all around you.

Rosa too cries out—she is hit in the foot. You pick her up and carry her out of range.

The next day, the Red Palace is deserted. All of your friends there have either been killed, arrested, or have fled the country.

→ → → → → → → → → → → →

Go on to the next page.

Rosa gets treatment for her foot at the hospital where she works and studies. You go there to see her before heading for the train station for your trip home—you've decided to quit the French Intelligence.

"It's so sad that people like Sergei have to die," Rosa says. "I hope something good comes out of this revolution, so that idealists like him will not have died for nothing."

"I hope so, too," you say. And you really mean it. But only history will tell if you are right.

The End

You decide to check in at headquarters. You go back to the French embassy and down to your basement office. Brossard is there, buried as usual up to his neck in new reports.

"Laurentine has been looking for you," he says. "I think he has a special assignment for you."

"I knew it," you say. "I'm glad I don't have to stay down here in this dismal cave."

"Like me, you mean."

"No offense, Brossard," you say. "We're just cut from different cloth."

"Well, you'd better get your cloth up to Laurentine's office."

"All right, I'll see you later," you say.

"Ah, there you are," Laurentine says as you enter his office. "You're going to take a trip out of the city—to army headquarters at Mogilev."

"But I thought you needed me to keep tabs on the Bolsheviks here in Petrograd," you say.

"I do," Laurentine says. "But I also need you to find out what General Kornilov, the commander at the front, is up to. Brossard has been getting all sorts of conflicting reports. There are rumors that Kornilov is going to send troops to overthrow the provisional government and set himself up as dictator. Other rumors say that he might try to return the country to the control of the old regime, only without the czar. Above all, I need to know what he will do if the Bolsheviks take over."

"Can't you just talk to him on the telephone or—" you start.

"No, I need a personal emissary, and you've been elected. When you see Kornilov, give him this," Laurentine says as he hands you an envelope.

A staff car, waiting outside, drives you to Kornilov's personal armored train waiting on a siding just outside the city. It's filled with officers and a few regular soldiers, all returning to the front.

Eight hours later, you arrive at staff headquarters at Mogilev. There an adjutant meets you at the train and takes you directly to Kornilov's office. Kornilov opens the letter from Laurentine and reads it carefully. Then he sits back in his chair and sighs heavily.

"I know all about these rumors," Kornilov says. "That fool Kerensky is so paranoid that he believes everyone is plotting against him. I'm doing my best to keep things together here while the Germans constantly attack. But we're losing men by the millions. The rest are close to starvation and are almost out of ammunition. Morale is at its lowest point. And on top of everything, Kerensky supports an order from the provisional government that the soldiers can elect their own officers."

Kornilov jumps up and slams his fist on the desk in front of him. "How can I maintain discipline at the front with this sort of thing going on?"

"What about the Bolsheviks?" you ask.

"Ah, the Bolsheviks," Kornilov says, sitting down again. "Kerensky keeps threatening me with the Bolsheviks. He needn't worry. If the Bolsheviks do try to take over, I intend to send troops to the capital to restore the authority of the government. In fact, I'm about to send a detachment to the city to arrest Lenin and the other Bolshevik plotters. I have proof that they are nothing more than paid German agents, working to destroy the Russian fighting machine."

"I'm sure Monsieur Laurentine will be glad to hear that," you say.

→ → → → → → → → → → → → →

Go on to the next page.

"I'm sending the evidence in this envelope for you to take back to Laurentine," Kornilov says. "He'll know what to do with it."

You are escorted back to the train, where soldiers are lined up waiting to board. At least these soldiers look well fed and are well armed.

"These are the last of our elite troops," a smartly uniformed officer standing next to you says. "Perhaps they can prevent disaster in the capital."

"You mean keeping the Bolsheviks from taking power?" you ask.

"Yes, that and more. The officer corps is hoping that Kornilov will succeed Kerensky as president."

"In a military takeover?" you say.

"Nothing like that," the officer says. "It will be completely democratic. But first we must restore order."

You and the officer, whose name is Ivan, sit together on the train as it rumbles across the flat countryside. An hour or so later, it comes to a sudden stop.

"Something must be wrong!" Ivan exclaims, jumping up from his seat.

You look out the window and see the train's engineer and several crewmen running away as fast as they can across a broad field.

→ → → → → → → → → → → →

Go on to the next page.

You and Ivan get off the train. You are somewhere in the vastness of the Russian plain.

Ivan goes up along the train, giving orders to the troops to remain calm. Several minutes later he comes back.

"The brutes have marooned us out here in the middle of nowhere," he says. "They've sabotaged the engine."

"Where are we?" you ask.

"I have no idea," Ivan says. "There's no town, no roads, nothing in sight."

"It looks like the workers don't want you to get to Petrograd," you say.

"They've done a good job of it, I'll say that," Ivan says. "We're a two-week march at least from the city. By that time my troops will be all worn out."

Ivan picks out the most likely direction, and you and his troops start out. On the second day of the march, you stumble upon a vast estate with a large, luxurious mansion at its center. The owners have fled, and the estate has already been partially looted by the local peasants. It's requisitioned by Ivan for his troops.

There is no transport of any kind left, but there's plenty of food in the storehouse.

You spend the next few weeks at the estate, while the troops relax and enjoy themselves by swimming in a large lake situated on the property. They elect a new commanding officer—one in favor of staying there indefinitely. Ivan is de-moted back to the ranks, but he doesn't seem to mind.

Somehow, you don't relish getting back to the embassy either. Laurentine will be furious, and the political situation in Petrograd may be cha-otic, as well as dangerous. The revolution in Rus-sia, you think, will just have to wait for you to catch up with it—though in your heart you know it won't.

The End

Glossary

Anarchists—A political group that is opposed to any kind of government. They place an emphasis on violence and revolutionary action to destroy governmental control. They are also responsible for the assassination of many world leaders.

Bolsheviks—The Workers' Party led by Lenin and his fellow revolutionaries. They seized control of the government in October 1917, and then refused to share power with any other groups—suppressing all rival political organizations.

Capitalism—Often called "the free enterprise system." The system in which the means of production are privately owned and production and income distribution are guided by the function of free markets. Capitalism, for example, is the economic system of the United States of America.

Cossacks—These were originally members of a militant people living on the undeveloped frontiers of Russia. Later they provided military service to the czars in exchange for special privileges. The cossacks were used primarily in the nineteenth and early twentieth centuries to suppress revolutionary activities.

Czar (also spelled *tsar* or *tzar*)—A form of the imperial Roman title of "Caesar." Used as a title by the supreme rulers of Russia from the thirteenth to the early twentieth centuries. In their heyday the czars held absolute power but were completely overthrown in the Russian uprisings of 1917.

Feudalism—The system by which wealthy landlords exercised control over the peasantry. The peasants owned no land of their own and, though theoretically "free," were in *reality virtual slaves to their feudal masters.*

First World War (also called *World War I* or *the Great War*)—This war pitted the "Central Powers" —Germany, Austria-Hungary, and Turkey— against the "Allies"—France, Great Britain, Italy, Japan, and from 1917, the United States. It lasted from 1914 (shortly after a Serbian nationalist assassinated Archduke Ferdinand of Austria) until the Central Powers were completely defeated in 1918.

Kerensky, Aleksandr Fyodorovich (1881–1970)—A socialist politician of the moderate left, Kerensky supported Russian participation in the First World War (which Lenin opposed). After the czar was deposed, Kerensky was appointed vice chairman of the Petrograd Soviet. He was soon made minister of war, and finally prime minister of the provisional government. Kerensky tried to unite the disparate political factions but only succeeded in alienating most of them. The officer corp of the army felt him too liberal, and the left wing of his government attacked him for refusing to implement their more radical economic programs. Kerensky went into hiding when the Bolsheviks seized power, then emigrated to Western Europe in 1918, and to the United States in 1940.

Keshinskiya Palace—An elegant palace near the Neva River, originally the residence of the ballerina Matilda Keshinskiya, that served as headquarters for the Bolshevik Party during 1917. Lenin frequently addressed his followers here.

Kronstadt Naval Base—A fort and naval base built by Czar Peter the Great on an island near the head of the Gulf of Finland. It was designed to protect the approaches to St. Petersburg. The garrison there took part in the July 1917 mutiny against the provisional government and supported the Bolsheviks.

Lenin, Vladimir Ilyich Ulyanov (1870–1924)—Founder of the Russian Communist (Bolshevik) Party and principal leader of the Bolshevik Revolution of 1917.

Malevich, Kasimir (1878–1935)—The Russian painter who founded the suprematist school of abstract painting. His early work was influenced by the impressionists, but after a trip to Paris in 1912, he became interested in cubism and abstract painting. Malevich worked and taught in both Moscow and Leningrad (Petrograd). His famous *White on White* painting is displayed in the Museum of Modern Art in New York City.

Mensheviks—These were members of the Russian Social Democratic Party. Unlike the Bolsheviks, the Mensheviks wanted to establish a free, liberal, and capitalistic regime. After the October revolution of 1917 they attempted to set up a legal opposition but were permanently suppressed by the Communists.

Petrograd—This second-largest city in Russia is on the southern shore of the Gulf of Finland on the delta of the Neva River. It was founded by Czar Peter the Great in 1703 as his capital. He named it St. Petersburg. At the beginning of the First World War, the name was changed to Petrograd, and after the Russian Revolution it was changed again to Leningrad. The capital of the czars became the birthplace of the U.S.S.R. through the Russian Revolution. Just recently the city has been renamed St. Petersburg.

Red Army—Created by the Communists under the direction of Leon Trotsky after the Bolshevik Revolution. Initially, the Red Army was recruited exclusively from the workers and peasants.

Red Guards—Armed groups of radical factory workers that sprang into existence during the revolutions of 1917.

Reed, John (1887–1920)—Reed was a reporter for New York City newspapers as well as a revolutionary writer and radical activist. He was an eyewitness to the Russian Revolution in 1917 in Petrograd and wrote a book about it titled *Ten Days That Shook the World*. He died shortly afterward in Russia of typhus and is buried beside the Kremlin wall in Moscow.

Soviets—Parliaments elected by members of working-class organizations, such as the steelworkers, the peasants, and the common soldiers.

Stalin, Joseph Vissarionovich Dzhugashvili (1879–1953)—Originally trained for the priesthood, Stalin later joined the Bolsheviks as a fanatic revolutionary. He was a relatively minor figure before the revolution of 1917, but later seized control of the Communist Party.

Trotsky, Leon (Lev Davidovich Bronstein) (1879–1940)—One of the leaders of the October 1917 Revolution. Trotsky was later made commissar of foreign affairs and war. After Lenin's death in 1924, Trotsky and Stalin fought it out for the top position in the Communist Party. Trotsky lost and went into exile. He was later murdered in Mexico by an agent of Stalin.

Suggested Reading

If you enjoyed this book, here are some other books on Russia that you might like:

Fitzpatrick, Sheila. *The Russian Revolution*. Oxford: Oxford University Press, 1982. This is a comprehensive analysis of the Russian Revolution. It tells how the revolution was fed by great ideals, optimism, and hope, but betrayed in the end by the Bolsheviks.

Rosenstone, Robert A. *Romantic Revolutionary: A Biography of John Reed*. New York: Alfred A. Knopf, 1975. This biography traces John Reed from his youth in Oregon through his student days at Harvard University to his role as a larger-than-life character on the world scene. A dedicated revolutionary as well as a writer and reporter, he directly participated in the struggles of Pancho Villa, Lenin, and Trotsky.

Salisbury, Harrison E. *Russia in Revolution, 1900–1930*. New York: Holt, Rinehart & Winston, 1978. This coffee-table book gives a comprehensive portrait of the Russian Revolution. It stresses the work of the artists and designers who created new directions in art against the background of the revolution. It contains many illustrations, several full page and in color.

Schapiro, Leonard. *The Russian Revolutions of 1917: The Origins of Modern Communism*. New York: Basic Books, Inc., 1984. A definitive account of how the Bolsheviks seized power in 1917, and how they managed to hold on to that power in the face of the party's growing unpopularity.

Thompson, John M. *Revolutionary Russia, 1917*. New York: Charles Scribner's Sons, 1981. This book covers the major events of 1917 from the downfall of the czar to the coming to power of the Bolsheviks.

Wechsberg, Joseph. *In Leningrad*. New York: Doubleday & Co., Inc., 1977. The city has changed names many times—first St. Petersburg, then Petrograd, then Leningrad—and now back again to St. Petersburg. This book is a well-written blend of history and art appreciation, describing the art treasures, parks, and palaces and detailing their cultural backgrounds. It contains many full-page photos in both color and black-and-white.

ABOUT THE AUTHOR

RICHARD BRIGHTFIELD is a graduate of Johns Hopkins University, where he studied biology, psychology, and archaeology. For many years he worked as a graphic designer at Columbia University. He has written many books in the Choose Your Own Adventure series, including *Master of Kung Fu, Master of Tae Kwon Do, Hijacked!*, and *Master of Karate*. In addition, Mr. Brightfield is the author of the first two books in The Young Indiana Jones Chronicles series. He has also coauthored more than a dozen game books with his wife, Glory. The Brightfields and their daughter, Savitri, now live on the coast of southern Florida.

ABOUT THE ILLUSTRATOR

FRANK BOLLE studied at Pratt Institute. He has worked as an illustrator for many national magazines and now creates and draws cartoons for magazines as well. He has also worked in advertising and children's educational materials and has drawn and collaborated on several newspaper comic strips, including *Annie* and *Winnie Winkle*. He has illustrated many books in the Choose Your Own Adventure series, most recently *The Lost Ninja, Daredevil Park, Kidnapped!, The Terrorist Trap, Ghost Train*, and *Magic Master*. He is also the illustrator of the first two books in The Young Indiana Jones Chronicles series. A native of Brooklyn Heights, New York, Mr. Bolle now lives and works in Westport, Connecticut.